Dancing for England
74 collected poems

Melville Lovatt

TSL Publications

First published in Great Britain in 2022
By TSL Publications, Rickmansworth

Copyright © 2022 Melville Lovatt

ISBN / 978-1-914245-74-9

Front Cover image: https://pixabay.com

Melville Lovatt

Melville Lovatt was born in Bolton in 1948 and is an award-winning playwright, monologue writer and poet.

His work has been widely performed in smaller theatres throughout London.
- A number of his plays have won awards:
- 'The Powers That Be' won The Sussex Playwrights Club 1st Prize for best full-length play.
- 'Small Mercies, a full-length play, won The Jack Langford Memorial Award and the Derek Lomas Memorial Award.
- His one-act plays, 'The Grave' and 'The Kiss' were short-listed for the Diane Raffle Award.
- Two monologues from his 16-monologue collection 'Standing Alone', won The National Operatic & Dramatic Association London Region Performance Showcase Award in June 2018.

He is a three times winner of *The Harrow Times* Poetry Competition. *Dancing for England* is his first poetry collection to be published.

Melville Lovatt is a member of The Pinner Writers Group and past President of Harrow Writers Circle.

He lives in Hatch End, Northwest London.

By Melville Lovatt

FULL-LENGTH PLAYS

Small Mercies	Comedy-Drama	4M 2F
The Powers That Be	Thriller	3M 2F
Visiting Time	Family Drama	3M 2F
Desperate Measures	Dark Comedy	3M 1F

ONE ACT PLAYS

Accommodation	Tragicomedy	4M 1F
The Lamp	Comedy-Drama	1M 1F
The Distressed Table	Comedy Drama	1M 1F
The Boomerang	Comedy-Drama	3M 1Boy + Voiceover (F)
Making Adjustments	Comedy-Drama	1M 2F
The Kiss	Thriller	2M 1F
The Weekend	Drama	2M 1F
The Grave	Drama	2M

DUOLOGUE

Bedtime Story	Drama	1M 1F

4 SKETCHES & 2 MONOLOGUES

Bus Stop Blues	Comedy Drama	7M 3F

MONOLOGUE COLLECTIONS

Standing Alone	(16 Monologues)	8M 8F
Relationships	(6 Monologues)	3M 3F

(Relationships is a monologue anthology including 5 monologues from other writers.)

POETRY COLLECTIONS

Dancing for England	(74 Poems)

All enquiries to TSL Drama: www.tslbooks.uk

Contents

Poems Autobiographical?
Written during Lockdown, March 2020 – 2021

Three Poems Written before Lockdown – 2019

    (Alternative version of the Philip Larkin poem)

Acknowledgements

are due to the following in which a number of these poems first appeared:

The Harrow Times
The Barnet Borough Times
East Lane Theatre Scene Setter
Hatch End Arts Bulletin
Belmont Theatre Poetry Corner Newsletter
Sixty Plus Surfers Magazine

Dedication

To my wife Lynda, daughter Anna and son Simon.

Also to Barbara Towell for her wonderfully astute feedback support and the Pinner Writers Group for always being there.

Author's Introductory Note

I never thought I would write poetry again,
having stopped writing it, for personal reasons,
almost fifty years ago.
The first poem in this collection, 'To Poetry',
goes some way towards an explanation.

Although writing poetry in those early days
became too claustrophobic, it helped me to develop
a sense of timing and rhythm which I was able
to carry forward into other genres, particularly
playwriting and monologue writing.

To my own great surprise, 66 of these 74 poems
were written from March 2020, the beginning
of the Pandemic lockdown period.
(The Collection includes '7 Covid-19 Diary Poems.')

I lived the first 22 years of my life near Bolton, Lancashire,
before moving to London to study playwriting and take
advantage of the thriving Lunchtime Theatre Scene.
Just before Supermarkets appeared, my parents ran
a grocery shop which was very much the centre of the
community.
Since writing poetry again, I've found myself journeying back
in time.
Many of these poems spring from living in the north.

I hope I have succeeded in writing varied, accessible,
sometimes funny poems which can also be enjoyed
when read out loud.

Melville Lovatt 2022.

Introduction by NICK HORGAN, Poet.

Melville Lovatt's poems tell the tales of regret, relational tensions, second chances and occasional optimism, with nostalgia for ages past, and disappointment with the way things are. His characters are the people you know opened wide, and dealing with aging and retirement, resentment and reconciliation, with a shade of sharp humour here and there:

Our designer masks are a revelation!
Just choose one that's right for you.
Why not try a zebra or polka dot print?
Our leopard skin's proving popular too... (Behind the Mask.)

I've lost three golf games in a row
to my wife who I should defeat.
She makes sure all our friends find out.
'Have you lost again?' They tweet. (Retirement Games.)

Several poems address the pandemic, the fear and loss, and new behaviours, and the collection starts with two poems on his relationship with the words and poems themselves:

Already, I'd written myself into a corner,
imprisoned behind the blank sheet wall.
I had very little more to give.
Whatever was left, you demanded it all. (To Poetry.)

The majority of poems are written as narrative or in the first person, in a standard structure, which lend their own rhythm to the reader, with no tricky techniques to readjust to as each poem starts, giving the poems immediacy and accessibility. The variety of subjects is impressive – we have a mourner in a regrettable purple suit, dead wives speaking from beyond the grave advising their husbands on dating, and a salutary tale regarding the suitability of hamsters as pets are among the 74 poems.

Lovatt successfully deals with inner emotions and the voice inside one's head, the cumulative shaping of relationships over time, and accurate depictions of times gone by.

Highly enjoyable and very memorable.

To Poetry

I loved you dearly when I was young,
reading three volumes of poems each week.
In the barren desert of a northern town
you quenched my thirst. You let me speak.

But I couldn't follow down the darker lanes
you were leading me through. A voice said, 'No!
What will you write if you go through there?
More claustrophobic tales of woe?'

Already, I'd written myself into a corner,
imprisoned behind the blank sheet wall.
I had very little more to give.
Whatever was left, you demanded it all.

So, I abandoned you, but you wouldn't go.
You refused to be rejected.
Your shadow lingered over my plays.
Now you've fully returned, unexpected.

So many years after our first affair…
Will we do better, this time around?
Am I better equipped to cope with your ways?
Has a love, almost lost, been re-found?

Winning poem.
Harrow Times Poetry Writing Competition
May 2021

Words

Sometimes you arrive so fancy free,
so perfectly formed, so rhythmically right.
'How could you fail to trust me?' you ask.
'I'm *yours*. Not just some fly by night.

Look here,' you say, 'I'm all you've got.
Shakespeare knew this. Hitler too.
A force for good? Or evil? Which?
Decide before the night is through.'

A shaky premise! You know full well.
The choice so simple or so stark?
Between your *good or evil* stance
the world is neither light or dark.

'*Trust me*. What's your problem?' you ask.
'You know I'll never let you down.
I'm here to do just as you wish.
Are you a writer or just a clown?

I'll sing and dance, do whatever you want.
Paint pictures of a beautiful bay?
Or, should you want something in between,
you know you only have to say…'

Words, please go. I'm weary, now,
of your taunting, slippery seductive ways.
Tomorrow, we'll dance together again,
on and on to the end of my days.

3 EARLY POEMS 1967 – 1969

Tormentor

A Soccer Match dying

Separation

Tormentor

Old and crabbed in a squinting sun
he catwalks down my vision's aisle,
darkening every youthful corridor
with peevish tongue and vulture smile.

Like so many grey old men
breathing on for moans or prying,
poisoned by a waiting time
of wanting death though not the dying,

he claims his image demands respect,
is quite inevitably correct,
my inheritance awaiting.

I hate him. He thrives on small depressions.

Any cosier visions of an ancient self,
strangely alert, eccentric and kind,
sporting trendy jacket and pants,
with adoring young wife to cheer body and mind,
are always reduced to a whimsical blur
by something lurking, deep in his stare.

A Soccer Match Dying

A lone swallow in a sagging sky
still jet fights steely sulking clouds
as the hour accepts a shabby death.

The players still search
one scrambled goal.
One spark to blaze.

Long since a dripping
sardined crowd
hastened to a slow sure handclap.

The quicksand mud is winning.
Everywhere the smirking clock.
Both teams sink further from their dream.

Twenty minutes remain.
The gates blast wide but nobody leaves.
A thousand more thrill seekers swell the terrace
as the swallow through some enveloping aisle
retreats to search elsewhere the sun.

Finalist. *The Harrow Times* Poetry Writing Competition
21st March 2015

Separation

Each has lived alone some thirty years
since the day they parted without any tears.
Yet she still hears his foot on the stair
and he still smells his youth in her hair
and she still sails the seas of his eyes
lying shipwrecked on the shores of her thighs.

SEVEN COVID DIARY POEMS
March 2020 – April 2021

When All This Is Over

Boxed In

Behind the Mask

Street Walking

The Last Sale

Sales 2020 – A Call to Arms

The Fallen

When All This Is Over

When all this is over, we'll have a party.
The biggest party the world has seen.
If there's any money left, there'll be no expense spared.
We'll send out an invitation to the Queen.
And people will rejoice at still being alive.
They'll boogie all night and twist and jive
and do all kinds of dances they've never done before.
The lions in Trafalgar Square will roar
and even old Nelson will applaud and smile
for anyone going that extra mile,
helping golden oldies in isolation.
Oh! What a joy! What a celebration!

And when the party's finally over,
still mourning the thousands of loved ones lost,
will we vow to try and be different, then?
Giving more of ourselves, never counting the cost?

Winning Poem. *The Harrow and Barnet Times*
June 2020 Poetry Writing Competition.

Boxed In

The lockdown's entered week ten, now.
My hair again needs to be cut.
We're taking short walks every day,
trying hard not to get in a rut.

Though Monty Don we'll never be,
we're tending our garden much more,
reshaping borders, sowing seeds,
planting pretty flowers by the score.

On Thursday evenings we meet in our Close
to clap for the NHS.
Though we're doing our best to boost morale,
we're aware we could hardly do less.

When *will* this end? We ask ourselves.
Is the science really so sound?
Will the economy ever revive?
Will a vaccine ever be found?

We have no option: Try to survive.
The alternative? Suicide? – Madness?
With almost 40 thousand dead,
we feel anger and great sadness.

Our doorbell rings between 8 and 9.
Outside is the Tesco van.
We unpack our box of groceries now,
just grateful that we can.

25th May 2020

Behind the Mask

When visiting supermarkets or shops,
the Government's decreed a mask *must* be worn
until we have Covid under control.
Until a new vaccine is born.

Our designer masks are a revelation!
Just choose one that's right for you.
Why not try a zebra or polka dot print?
Our leopard skin's proving popular, too.

You know it makes sense. Don't make a fuss.
Wearing a mask can save your life.
To social distance – much more fun.
Why not treat your girlfriend or wife?

For casual wear, we've fantastic ranges.
For Indian weddings as well…
All our masks have special nose clips attached,
and every mask comes with free hand gel!

So, cheer up, now, and rest assured
there's no need to live under a cloud.
Our colorful masks will brighten your day,
really make you *stand out* in the crowd!

Runner Up Poem. *The Harrow and Barnet*
August 2020 Poetry Competition.

*28th August 2020. An Israeli jeweler has created a golden
diamond encrusted mask, said to be worth £1.5 million.

Street Walkers

Like prisoners trudging round their yard,
we walk each day at three o'clock.
Suburban streets are well-worn, now.
We know each house around the block.

They stare back, blank, but seem to ask,
'Who *are* these people walking past?
Do they know no *other* walks?
Why *are* they looking so downcast?'

The daily news, in sombre tones
proclaims a record number dead.
As NH troops fight bravely on,
the virus fills their every bed.

But could it be the end's in sight?
Will vaccine clinics win the day?
Despite new Covid Variants,
a total cure is on its way?

As grudging clouds begin to part,
forced to allow small rays of light,
we hurry home through spiteful wind
and lock our doors against the night.

19/01/2021

The Last Sale

The Winter Sales are here again.
Time for a treat. There are bargains galore.
But hurry! These wonderful deals won't last,
and when they're gone, there'll be no more.

This shop is finally closing down
after trading more than a hundred years.
Twin villains, Covid and 'Online'
have brought forth with them, bitter tears.

From our staff room wall, above the fire,
our Founder's face stares down.
If *he* were here, he'd find a way
to turn our shop around!

I'm afraid we staff know all too well,
when the battle's over, we'll count the cost.
Rampaging shoppers will give no thought
to fallen troops whose jobs are lost.

But still, we'll strive to give our best.
When we open our doors, this place will sing
with a shopping experience second to none.
Down all the years, our tills will ring.

Winning Poem. *The Harrow and Barnet Times*
December 2020 Poetry Writing Competition.

Sale Time 2020 – a Call to Arms

The shops have re-opened! There are bargains galore!
Come in and see what we have for you!
It's just as exciting as before the pandemic.
Our offers will stop you feeling so blue.

Why not treat yourself to a cashmere coat?
Or, for casual wear, some designer jeans?
You'll surely find something to suit your taste,
whatever your current financial means.

What's that? Oh dear, you've lost your job?
Your business has gone down the pan?
Well, we've cut our prices to the bone
to help out as much as we possibly can.

Even the rich are feeling the pinch.
Arcadia's collapse has left us stunned.
Someone's now faced with making good
the big black hole in the pension fund.

If it isn't made good, a *knighthood* may go!
This is surely no time to gloat.
Rally round our remaining High Street shops
and SPEND to keep us afloat!

December 2020

The Fallen

Strong linear stories are offered by wars
of causes, effects, famous battles galore.
Of intrigue, betrayal, strategic retreats,
victories, heroism much to the fore.

In each war, enemies are clearly defined.
Regardless of how many people have died,
we convince ourselves our cause is just,
continue fighting with God on our side.

Distant battles are recalled each year
at War Memorials throughout the land.
The Last Post sounds its solemn praise.
To honour the fallen, in silence we stand.

But what of those fallen in this Pandemic?
To Covid-19, its clutch so vile?
Will *their* names be carved on monuments, too?
Will they be remembered in similar style?

Their memory will always remain in our hearts,
outraged by this invisible foe
which denies the dying the right to hug,
to say goodbye before they go.

04/02/2021

POEMS WRITTEN DURING LOCKDOWN
March 2020 –2021

Dancing for England
At the Seaside
Moving Out
The Man in the old TV Ad
Action Man
Her Last Command
Why's Daddy Sleeping on the Sofa?
Going Back
For the Children's Sake
Taking Back Control
Penalty Shoot-Out 11/07/2021
Leaving St Kilda. August 29th 1930
None of His Business
Washington Assault 06/01/2021
The Accessory
Sleeping Dogs
Too Far Away
Flowers
The Kite
The Voice
Under the Anesthetic
Senior Moment
Away with the fairies
The Phone Call
Retirement Games
The Date
His Final Trip
Swimming against the Tide
The Young Vicar
Redundant
Walking the Dog

The Dance of Life
Conversation with the Thames on Waterloo Bridge
The Widow
A Day in the Care Home
The Happy Haven
From the Balcony
The Purple Suit
The Laughing Clown
The Mourner
At the Tea Dance
Santa's Story
Our Neighbour's Snowman
Black Cats
The Grand Old Duke of York Nursery Rhyme Revisited

Dancing for England

His wife and he both agree
she tends to know what's best.
She states precisely what she wants.
He adheres to her request.

Amazingly, she knows the words
he'll speak before they're uttered.
Her telepathic powers ensure
he's muted – mind uncluttered.

But tonight, their roles will be reversed.
Tonight, they'll rock 'n' roll.
They'll do their horizontal dance,
himself in full control.

She'll dance to *his* tune, no mistake.
They have a fresh understanding.
Wednesday – they're dancing in front of the fire.
Friday – the kitchen or landing.

Having lived through many ups and downs,
they're enjoying this time best,
now on a re-discovery path
since their children flew the nest.

She decided their long relationship
lacked sparkle, was losing its fizz.
This new routine was her idea
but she lets him think it's his.

So off they go to fight their foes;
Ageing and the passing of time.
Two tiny blue pills aid both of them
plus one small glass of wine,

and soon they'll be dancing, almost as if
their youth never slipped away.
Dancing for England twice a week,
the enemy kept at bay.

At the Seaside

Side by side in deckchairs they sit,
her dozing. Him staring out to sea
wondering where all the years have gone.
She dreaming of being young and free.

She once had her pick of handsome men.
Who *is* this stranger in the next chair,
overweight and bald as a coot?
Time for a change? Another affair?

So many beautiful women on the beach
flutter past him, bikini clad.
The blonde one seems to give him the eye…
But he's old enough to be her dad…

At twenty-three, she was often told
she looked like Marilyn Monroe.
So many men fell for her charms…
One even begged to suck her toe!

A petite brunette paddles in the sea,
definitely looking his way.
Irresistibly drawn to 'more mature' men,
her eyes are saying, 'Come in and play.'

She *could* have had her pick of the bunch!
If only her heyday would come again…
He decides to take a paddle, too…
But against all odds, it starts to rain.

Hardly getting wet, they make it back
to their hotel, quite close by.
A game of Bingo in the lounge,
then steak and kidney pie…

They both change clothes. She wears a dress.
She thinks his blazer, dashing.
He thinks her dress a little tight,
but her legs, they still look smashing.

In a quaint bar overlooking the sea,
They share a bottle of wine.
A marvelous tonic, the crisp sea air!
Now both are feeling fine.

She sees him in the different light
of love. There's still a glimmer.
She seems much younger to him, now,
more vibrant and much slimmer.

Perhaps, after all, everything's not lost?
Will it do the trick, this seaside break?
This very last throw of the dice?
They'd try once more. So much at stake…

Moving Out

He *had* to go. She'd had all she could take.
Asking him to move in was her biggest mistake.
He, of course taking a different view,
was delighted to be moving out, too.

Now, she sadly recalled, once things had been fine,
and she'd found him quite sexy – even sublime!
He'd been masterful, inventive in bed…
But to brewers droop, all his drinking had led.

He'd wasted, on her, three years of his life.
Thank God he'd never made her his wife!
Financially, he'd been brought to his knees.
She seemed to think money grew on trees!

If not a new kitchen --- exotic cats!
Teeth whitening, expensive dresses and hats…
It really was time to seek pastures anew,
his escape from her being long overdue.

Now she fleetingly wondered would she *ever get*
to be more astute when choosing her men?
She'd got it wrong so many times.
Would she learn from this and try again?

Life was a lottery, he told himself.
Some day he would win, not lose.
He'd win next time. Find someone new,
regain control and beat the booze.

On leaving, he felt great to be freed.
She thought, *at last, I no longer need
put up with his snoring and farting all night.*
She lay back, relieved, and put out the light.

The Man in the Old Tv Ad

The debonair man lit up his pipe,
face aglow with a satisfied smile.
Strolling leisurely towards his gated villa,
the smell of his pipe and a nonchalant style

made gorgeous women go weak at the knees
and follow him to his nest.
He allowed *one* woman inside the gates,
then kindly dismissed the rest.

Why had this never happened to him?
He had smoked St Bruno too!
If only life was an old TV ad
where fantasies all came true…

His smoking had only drawn complaints
when *he* lit up with a smile.
Instead of turning women on,
it had made them run a mile!

His wife had issued an ultimatum:
'Either your pipe goes or I do!'
In an ideal world, he'd have chosen his pipe
but his wife had…well…some *good* points too…

Right now, he couldn't really think of any
but he guessed she must have some…
'What about this sink? Have you cleared the drain?
Come on! Get up off your bum!'

Why couldn't he be the man in the ad,
 if only for just one day?
 Her voice was sounding angrier, now.
 He had better go in and obey.

Action Man

The newspaper ad asked, *'Is your life
marred by unsightly nasal hair?'*
A glance in the mirror confirmed the worst:
A dreaded forest was growing there!

He faced the truth. His life *was* marred.
He decided *this* was mainly to blame.
His lack of success with women due
to his naughty nostrils not playing the game.

Decisive action was needed now.
Simply no time for further delay.
This nostril shaver – free battery, too –
would herald the start of a brand-new day!

And so, when next he ventured forth,
not a single hair could be viewed.
He felt a new spring in his step,
his confidence fully renewed.

Though women still didn't fall at his feet,
with this wonderful number one trimmer
the balance was tipped in his favour, now.
He *knew* he was on to a winner…

Her Last Command

It was never meant to be like this.
He thought that he'd go first.
His health was never as good as hers…
Early evenings were the worst

when fragile light gave way to dark
he felt so much alone.
Was it really worth him going on?
'Course it is!' He heard her groan.

'Get off your bum. Don't sit and mope.
Try the internet to make a date.
It's no betrayal, now I'm dead.
Meet someone else – It's not too late.'

On hearing this, he ventured forth
to obey her last command.
Against all odds, to his surprise,
he seemed in great demand!

Why women flock to an older man,
he was never really sure.
Could his house, now mortgage-free,
add to his allure?

He'd found a new spring in his step
until her voice pricked like a pin;
'STOP enjoying yourself so much!'
He knew then, he could never win.

Why's Daddy Sleeping on the Sofa?

She hardly speaks to him at all
when he comes in at the end of the day.
His meal's always ready as before,
but he eats in silence. She's making him pay.

He's said he's sorry a thousand times.
Too much to drink… must have been mad
to risk their love for a stupid fling,
destroying her trust. All that they had.

A thousand times too, she's asked herself:
Can I forgive him? Make a new start?
Put all this behind us? Begin again?
Or is it simply better to part?

Careless betrayal, she knows can happen.
With sex, men are so easily led…
Should she keep him sleeping on the sofa?
Will she ever want him back in bed?

'Why's Daddy sleeping on the sofa?'
He hears his youngest son exclaim.
If only he could turn back time…
Will things ever be the same?

Going Back

As he stood before her modest house,
it seemed to whisper in his head;
'Go on, just knock. What can you lose?'
Came a louder voice: *'Oh no, she's dead.'*

'You don't know that. How can you know?'
'If she's still alive, she's eighty-two!
Do you really want to see her now?
She still has twenty years on you.

No point in going back in time.
Good memories should be left intact.
Why let the present wipe them out?
Sometimes it's better not to act.'

And so, he turned and walked away,
as he'd done so long ago.
The louder voice prevailed again,
seemed to mock, *'I told you so.'*

But he was happy, was he not?
To find a woman, more his age?
Two sons. Nice house. Promotion, car…
In full control at every stage…

The train came, late, to take him home.
As weary passengers pushed and shoved,
he wondered if he had betrayed
the only woman he had really loved.

For the Children's Sake

They argue far less than before.
A baffling silence prevails instead.
'For the children's sake,' they both agreed,
'we'll stay together.' – Or so they said…

So, what binds them on this day,
their children having flown the nest?
The main excuse for staying put
gone to Uni, east and west?

Is the villain 'force of habit?'
Better the Devil you know?
Or the mortgage rope around their necks,
still too tight to let them go?

What *is* the glue that holds them fast,
entering this strange new zone?
Could it be, the dye is cast,
both too afraid to be left alone?

Or could it be there's still a thread
of love and shared history?
On this they reflect and ponder now –
life's unfurling mystery.

Taking Back Control

350 mil a week to the NHS?
I'm afraid, well…Covid's scuppered all that…
Cheer up. We're taking back control.
We're at the crease. *Our* turn to bat.

What's that? You were promised a brand-new car?
Been sold an old banger instead?
Well, sacrifices have to be made
If we want to get ahead…

Come on, don't sulk. You know it makes sense --
always some darkness before the light…
brief suffering first… small price to pay…
look, rest assured, our futures bright.

We'll stand unshackled. On our own two feet--
forget the fishermen! --- wait and see,
our country's pride will be restored.
We'll know what it means to be *really* free!

Free from the threat of more immigration!
Free from the tyranny of the E U!
Free from Financial Regulation!
From all the meddling Unions too!

The morning's coming! A brand-new dawn!
Once more we'll play a *major* role.
We'll be the *envy* of the world
for finally taking back control!

The Penalty Shoot-out
11/07/2021

On steel wings, extra time has flown.
A brutal shoot-out will decide
whose cup will overflow with joy
or heartbreak if their dream has died.

The ball is placed upon the spot.
A terrible silence starts to reign.
The penalty taker, about to strike,
will release great roars of triumph or pain.

The goalie…will he be the hero?
From his line, alone and brave,
will he turn the odds around?
Read the striker's mind, and save?

For the striker, there is all to gain.
More to lose if he should miss.
No mercy or solace for him *then*.
Small comfort in a pitying kiss.

Will football history now be made?
The referee's whistle, sharp and shrill,
propels the striker towards his goal.
The crowd awaits the final kill.

Leaving St Kilda
August 29th 1930

What did they think and feel as they left?
A sense of an ending? Sadness? Defeat?
Or a sense of adventure? Relief? Escape?
A new beginning? A challenge to meet?

A chance to explore a different world,
whilst living in Glasgow's tenement blocks?
Wide open spaces, hills and grass
replaced by factory, shipyard, docks?

Old photos offer no real clues.
Stoic faces stare back, dead
to any hint of hardships past
or changes lying just ahead.

At 8 a.m., they made their move.
No livelihood – no sense in staying.
As they sailed on HMS *Harebell*
did it seem a price worth paying?

As seabirds circled overhead,
screeching their forlorn goodbye,
St Kilda, fading out of view,
in their hearts would never die.

None of His Business

None of his business when the roundups started
and they came and took his neighbour away.
*'For spreading lies about the State
on social media,'* he heard them say.

None of his business when the roundups continued,
targeting minority groups.
How could *he* be blamed for any of this?
Wasn't down to *him*, them sending troops…

None of his business. The important thing was to
keep his head down. Get on with his life.
Why *should* he get involved at all?
Who needs this extra struggle and strife?

None of his business when they knocked on
his door and took his wife and son away?
'What have they done that's so wrong?' he asked.
'We'll tell you later,' he heard them say.

Washington Assault
06/01/2021

'Freedom! Freedom! Freedom!' They shout.
'Stop the steal! Stop the steal!
Our country! *Our* country! We want it back!
Trump WON the vote for a better deal!'

Much reduced in number since Black Lives Matter,
Police hover, bewildered, dejected.
Helpless to stop the raging mobs
their Chief said were never expected.

Though proof of fraud there's never been,
the mob's convinced it has the right
to overturn Joe Biden's vote
and force him to give up the fight.

Meanwhile, from The White House, crocodile tears
condemning the violence, flow like piss.
'Incitement? – Such an unpleasant word.
We certainly never expected this…'

Democracy fragile, a bullied child,
lies weeping in the sack,
nursing a swollen, bloody nose,
knowing the bully will soon be back.

The Accessory

Two men sipping their beer, Bishops Finger.
Something about them made him linger.
With Sunday Times concealing his head,
he could hear quite clearly what they said:

'Shall I use a shooter or a blade?
Your choice. You're paying me, Jed.'
'How you do it is up to you.
Tonight, I just want him dead.'

'In that case, I'll just use my gun.
No worries. Job's as good as done.
As for his body, it'll just disappear.
They'll never find it, have no fear.'

The Police Station was across the road…
He *had* to do what he thought was right…
Reporting precisely what he'd heard
may prevent a murder this very night.

Out of the blue, a friend then appeared.
'It's my birthday. Tonight, all drinks are on me.'
Though he pleaded, *'Have to go very soon…'*
Somehow, he found he couldn't break free.

He remained, now, until closing time.
The two men? – They didn't stay.
He hoped that soon the guilt he felt,
like snow would melt away.

Sleeping Dogs

Her voice is ever present, now,
in his prison cell. It echoes '*Why?*'
He's shown remorse a thousand times,
begging her, '*Let sleeping dogs lie.*'

All this had happened a lifetime ago!
He had thought she was eighteen at least.
Had no idea she was under-age
until their frantic sex had ceased

and she, not wanting it to end,
threatened then to tell his wife.
Came other threats, involving police...
For this, she paid with her life.

Now her ageless face appears again
as she taunts him, laughing through each day,
'*For thirty years, you thought you were safe?*
Too bad you hadn't reckoned with DNA.'

Too Far Away

Frank Morris, who lived facing
in a terraced house like his own,
spent weeks, now, sitting, staring out
from a window, by the phone.

For years, he'd been used to seeing
each day, a jogging, cycling Frank.
A fitness freak (if that's the word)
who neither smoked or drank.

How come, then, this sudden change?
Frank sitting like a stone,
just gazing into outer space,
so distant? So alone?

Perhaps he should go across the road,
knock on Frank's front door?
Enquire about the state of play
and *help*, not just ignore?

'I'll do it.' He firmly decided,
but from somewhere came a cry:
*'You really don't know Frank too well.
It's not your place to pry.'*

'Nothing to be done.' Words from
'Waiting for Godot' rang clearly in his ear.
Frank could surely manage his own affairs?
'Forget it, now! Don't interfere...'

'Misadventure,' the newspaper said
three months later. *Not suicide.*
For the following week, he asked himself
Could he have helped to turn the tide?

But to his relief, the answer came back,
'Nothing to be done at the end of the day.'
The simple facts were, when all's said and done,
some people are just...too far away.

Flowers

Someone had come before him,
put flowers on her grave.
He puzzled as to who this was…
Her brothers, Chris or Dave?

No, it couldn't be those two.
They lived too far away…
It must be someone nearer home…
But who? He dared not say.

He'd often wondered how they'd
stayed together through the years.
Just force of habit? No. Not true.
They'd *loved* through joy and tears.

But the flowers provoked a vision, now:
His son's face, crystal clear.
The same face, yes, of best friend, Jim.
A shadow fell, quite near…

Could it be true, he had *always* known?
Played along for appearances sake?
Had Jim, a married man, known too?
Too much had been at stake?

Through angry tears, he grabbed the flowers,
and threw them in a bin.
A man was closing the cemetery gates.
Better go or be locked in…

Runner Up. July 2020
The Harrow and Barnet Times Poetry Competition.

The Kite

'It's over,' she said, standing by the window.
'Whatever we had together, it's gone.
There's not much left between us, now.
It's over. Time to just move on.'

On the beach below, as she spoke,
a man was running, flying a kite.
'Make it go faster!' Children cried.
'Make it go higher!' The sun shone bright.

Her words, exploding in his head,
lit up the wreckage of his life.
Other earlier voices repeated her words,
sank in deeply like a knife.

Yet again, another failed love affair.
Where would he move to this time around?
Was he really *meant* to live alone?
The kite was diving to the ground.

'That's not the case!' Another voice.
'Each woman's different than before.'
The kite was flying up again
as she said goodbye and closed the door.

The Voice

Never one of those silly fools
who thought they had endless time,
he always knew, come one dark day,
his poem would strain to rhyme.

'But could you have taken a different road?'
The voice sounded in his head.
'No matter, now it's far too late.
Your chance has gone. You'll soon be dead.'

Where did it come from, this taunting voice
which plagued him night and day?
Though he tried so hard to shut it out,
it refused to go away.

'You married the wrong woman.
You failed to gain promotion.
Your children never speak to you.
Your life's one long commotion.

I hesitate to use the word,
but failure comes to mind.
What happened to all those dreams you had?
I hate to sound unkind...'

Would he *ever* be able to silence the voice?
Could he even keep it at bay?
To make it go away for good,
what price would he have to pay?

Under the Anesthetic

Now he was a boy of six again.
'Your Grandma's gone to God,' mum said.
They stared at grandma in her box,
the first time he'd seen someone dead.

In the front parlour, she lay in state.
His mum had made him say goodbye.
He couldn't believe gran was *really* dead.
She'll soon wake up. He didn't cry.

Why was he seeing grandma, *now*?
Was he close to death, himself?
Though at fifty, he *felt* in reasonable shape,
he was hardly a picture of health…

Perhaps he was already dead,
if death was a limbo to last?
His pieces of memory failing to fit
the crazy jigsaw of his past?

He stared down from the ceiling
at himself, now twelve years old,
a sea of white coats all around,
sun flooding the room with gold…

He wanted to stay forever, there.
No desire for any release…
But a soft voice sounded in his ear…
'You're luckily still in one piece.'

'Ready, now, for a nice cup of tea?'
The nurse was helping him sit up in bed.
How good it felt to be alive,
to face the twisting road ahead.

Senior Moment

It *had* to be here, in Morrisons car park!
Where did he park it? *Concentrate!*
Was it over near the trolley shed,
or further away, by the exit gate?

The trouble was, a thousand cars
all looked just like his own.
Relax. Stay calm, he told himself.
It's not just *you* – you're not alone.

A Senior Moment, that's all this is.
He'd coped with worse things in his life...
But how long had this search gone on?
He wondered – should he phone his wife?

No! Don't do that! She'll get alarmed.
She'll only fuss and fret.
He had to sort this out, himself,
not make her more upset.

Then suddenly, the solution came!
Simply click on his ignition key!
His car would flash a guiding light;
take him home, in time for tea.

But no key from his pocket came.
Memory flickered from a darkened wood.
He had left the car back on his drive,
thinking the walk would do him good.

Away with the Fairies

Why are they staring at him like this?
Was he *so* different from yesterday?
Their eyes proclaim there's something wrong.
'Away with the fairies,' he heard them say.

Why this changing sea of faces
dancing forever around his bed?
Two clear voices in his ear…
'Dad, we're your children, Ann and Ted.'

Their names mean nothing. Ring no bells.
Down crumpled faces more tears flow.
'Try to remember, Dad,' they say.
They kiss his cheek and turn to go.

A white-coated man is shaking his head.
This surely must be a dream?
Was he so different from yesterday?
What does, 'away with the fairies,' mean?

The Phone Call

The telephone plucked him from a sexy dream.
Erotic fragments in seconds fled
away from his memory into thin air.
Too much wine, again. He'd a terrible head.

What idiot rings at this time of night?
Whatever it was, he was sure it could wait.
Could a guy *never* get a decent night's sleep?
He glared at the phone with considerable hate.

Letting it ring, he turned over in bed.
Told himself, soon the ringing would cease.
Just give it a minute. Two minutes max…
He was right. It stopped. Now, silence. Peace!

But it rang again, a minute later!
He shouted, grabbing throat of the phone,
'HELLO?! WHO IS IT?! WHAT DO YOU WANT?!'
This different silence said, 'You're alone.

I'm afraid it's the end of the line, old son.
You've run your last race. Your battery's flat.
This time, next year, you won't be around.
Have you made a will? Should think about that…'

'I'm not alone!' he yelled down the phone.
'*I have a faith! Have God on my side!*'
"*Well, where is he, now?*' the silence asked.
He's here somewhere…somewhere…' he sighed.

'*Besides, I have regular check-ups as well.*
For high cholesterol, prostate, heart…
Rest assured, you bastard, I'm not going yet.
On your bike, old son! Your turn to depart!'

Tomorrow, this ancient phone he'd give the boot.
Who needs a landline? Come what may,
he'd treat himself to a high-spec phone…
A Full English Breakfast to start the day…

Retirement Games

It's true, I always play to win.
The fact is – I hate losing.
To continue losing to my wife?
Too much to bear! Confusing…

When we retired, 'Sports!' I suggested
as a way of keeping fit.
I thought I'd let her win sometimes.
Now I'm looking such a twit.

I've lost three golf games in a row
to my wife who *I should* defeat.
She makes sure all our friends find out.
'Have you lost again?' They tweet.

She's beating me at badminton.
At table tennis as well.
My good intentions, suggesting sports,
have paved the road to hell.

Introducing ten pin bowling was
my worst mistake, it's true.
The tenpin bowl slipped from her hand…
Now I'm wearing a plaster shoe.

Meanwhile, she's having *more* golf lessons
with her handsome instructor, Ron.
I'm starting to think that all's not right.
There's something going on…

The Date

At last, all his trouble was rewarded.
With chocolates, flowers, he knocked on her door.
Unexpectedly, she'd invited him round
for a meal at her house and…something more?

Her suggestion was *most* agreeable
in view of his present financial state.
A meal in a pricey restaurant? No…
Her house – *much* better for a first date…

He rang the bell once, stood waiting a while.
He rang again when the moment felt right.
She was making him wait a little, that's all…
Just teasing him. Whetting his appetite…

It really had been a very long time
since wife Amy died. Yes, nearly ten years.
He had never thought of finding new love…
Now grieving was done. He had shed his tears.

The door opened. He was faced with two men.
He was punched in the stomach, heard himself groan.
They dragged him inside. *'We'll teach you a lesson.*
Teach you to leave a man's wife alone.'

The larger of the two held him down.
He was punched and kicked by the smaller lout.
Conscious of blood gushing onto his tie…
They picked him up and threw him back out.

He lay for a while, hardly conscious at all.
She'd just led him on. He'd followed – a fool,
been well and truly rewarded, now,
for breaking society's golden rule.

Now darkness fell. He limped in the dark
towards a small ball of light ahead.
The light grew no nearer as he went on…
Was he still alive? Or was he dead?

Where was he, now? In a tunnel of sorts?
A tunnel? *'GET A GRIP!'* He screamed out.
Surely his memory would soon return?
Come on, son! What is all this about?!

'Don't panic,' he told himself. 'Just keep moving.'
Any time, now, he would reach the light...
He would get his bearings once and for all.
'Stay positive. POSITIVE! JUST STAY BRIGHT!'

As a boy, he had gone through a tunnel
with another lad, playing some sort of game.
Not a tunnel. A cave...he'd ended up lost.
His parents were frantic, calling his name.

'Daniel! Where are you?!' Other voices joined in.
'Daniel! Daniel!' The chorus grew.
It had seemed, *then,* he would never be found...
But he *was* found. Now, they'd find him too.

He'd be back with Amy – no time at all.
How he loved her, more than ever before.
'Keep moving! Keep moving!' His legs, so tired...
'The light's getting nearer. A few steps more...'

'Okay, it's all over.' The white coated doctor's
voice reassured at the end of the bed.
*'Believe me, you've had a lucky escape.
They beat you up badly, left you for dead.'*

The telephone rang, plucked him out of his dreams
'Hello, it's me' – a voice just like the Queen's...

*'Hello, it's me. About our date tonight?
I've been thinking about it. What's the big deal?
Restaurants are expensive. Was wondering if you'd prefer
to come here? I could make us a meal...'*

His Final Trip

He had made up his mind. His time had come *now*.
He'd drive off the cliff, straight into the sea.
He'd flirted, briefly, with other ways out:
Jump under a train? Find a suitable tree...?

But no, this way out was best by far.
A spectacular exit with *some* panache...
His Mercedes floating through the air...
His heart giving out, before the crash...

He decided on just one last cigarette.
(He'd tried to stop smoking without success.)
Well, *no more* failures, he told himself.
No more financial worries or stress...

Could things have been different? Too late, now.
Too many wrong turnings along the way.
Could he have taken *another* road?
There was nothing left to do or say.

A sudden bark from the car's back seat;
Max, awakening from a snooze.
Take his best friend with him or let him go?
Who'd look after his dog? It was time to choose.

Well, no, this didn't seem right at all.
He really needed to get a grip.
Find a caring person to look after Max.
Postpone until later, his final trip...

Swimming Against the Tide

Only when doing his weekly swim
could he find some sort of peace.
Swimming allowed his mind to roam free.
Made complaining voices cease.

Granted, his Customer Services job
meant complaints were his bread and butter.
Was he *really*, as his wife had claimed,
Just a masochistic nutter?

'You're suited to this job,' she hissed.
It satisfies your needs.
You know you like to suffer, so…
don't bite the hand that feeds.'

Professional Complainers were the worst…
They were, all of them, *real* turds.
For his wife to claim he *enjoyed* all this---
too ridiculous for words!

It suited her to think like this,
with her domineering ways…
He'd show her who was *really* boss
one of these fine days.

If only he could retire right now.
He'd not be shedding tears.
Only fifteen lengths to swim…
And another fifteen years…

The Young Vicar

Why was he chosen for this village church?
Why had the bishop sent him here?
He put some more wood on his fire.
Why he was chosen just wasn't clear…

Although no pin-up boy at all,
he struggled to keep his parish at bay.
Two particular women—spinsters, both---
chose to pursue him night and day.

Having no interest in amorous pursuits,
he tactfully tried to show them the door.
But his protestations only served
to make them want him all the more!

So much had gone wrong since he'd arrived.
A parishioner's dog had bitten his leg.
He dearly wanted to get a gun
and shoot the little ****** dead.

Of course, this was hardly Christian, he knew.
His leg now showed signs of healing.
He would give the dog a gentle pat
to show there was no hard feeling.

The truth of it was, he felt…alone.
Forsaken in this backwater church.
Prayed for heavenly guidance which never came…
The bishop had left him in the lurch.

Nothing for it but to soldier on…
Pray tomorrow his faith would return…
His Bible College seemed light years away.
He stoked his fire and watched it burn.

Redundant

Mr Glibb speaks softly, with a sympathetic smile,
'We have to let you go, I'm afraid.
It's no reflection on your skills.
You're highly thought of in the trade.

No, it's really just a sign of the times.
Technology – beyond our control…
Online shopping is here to stay.
High Street shopping? – No future role.'

He listened in silent fury
as Mr Glibb demolished his retail life.
'I'm afraid this is happening all over the world.'
How on earth would he tell his wife?

Take it on the chin, then? Stiff upper lip?
Or give full reign to helpless rage?
If only he were young again…
Too late to turn a different page…

The light outside was starting to fade
as he made his way to the station.
On the train home, his mood…it changed
from depression to brief elation.

At fifty–nine, he still had his health.
Happily married thirty-five years…?
Together, they'd ridden many storms.
They'd ride one more, find joy through tears.

Walking the Dog

At seventy, his memory's not all it was.
He ponders this, walking little dog, Rex.
Would remaining days all merge into one?
Always tease and tantalize? Worry? Perplex?

What did he actually *do* yesterday?
Get a grip. Try hard to remember!
Does he even know which month it is?
Is it August... or September?

My God, he thinks, it's getting worse.
Soon he won't remember his name.
Ever since his lovely wife had died,
things had never been the same...

Perhaps he should think of having a test
for Alzheimer's or even dementia?
Come on! The only thing *really* wrong
was his ill-fitting new top denture!

Much better to just soldier on.
The alternative to survival? Stark.
Why look for problems where there's none?
Now, little Rex began to bark...

Coming towards them was a burly man
with a very large Alsatian.
Though only standing ten inches tall,
fearless Rex loved confrontation.

But maybe that's what it's all about?
Never being afraid of what's ahead?
'The moment is really all you have.
Live in the moment,' a faint voice said.

The light, now, was beginning to fade.
A brief barking skirmish ensued.
All honour satisfied, man and dog
returned home, somewhat renewed.

The Dance of Life

Still she hears her husband's voice,
'Get out. Meet people. Find someone new.
Perhaps consider getting a dog?
When I'm dead, don't sit there, feeling blue.'

Now, he is and she's paying the price
of loving him for forty years.
'Remember the good times.' She tells herself
'The love and laughter. No more tears.'

Although she knows she *will* survive—
Alternative? Suicide? Madness? –
watching other couples dance,
she's overcome with sadness.

But knowing, now, that pain and joy
dance together – partners in crime –
She'll do the dance of life again
with both – just one more time.

Conversation with the Thames on Waterloo Bridge

'Why not join me? No more worries,'
Father Thames whispered from below.
'Ditch the wreckage of your life.
A greater peace, you'll never know.'

'But why *should* I throw in my hand
when all my cards have not been dealt?'
'Don't fool yourself. Your time is up.
Jump in — feel your sorrow melt.

You've no more cards. Your hand's complete.
Your final race is run.
I'm ready to embrace you, now.
All over soon…All done…'

'Tomorrow is another day…'
'Your life's a mess. Get real !'
'Still time to turn a different page…'
'Your wounds will never heal.'

A pavement beggar shouted, then;
'Sometimes, *all* of us cry!'
As he threw coins in the beggar's cap,
the Thames, forsaken, sulked on by.

The Widow

'Have you thought of joining The Women's Guild?
What about Yoga? Pilates? Tai Chi?
Get involved with the church more? Join the choir?
Well, that's what I'd do, if it were me.'

Their suggestions, they keep coming, non- stop.
Oh, people *mean well*, I suppose…
But as time's gone by— it's been a year ---
their *sympathy* gets up my nose.

Being married to Tom was no fairy tale.
You know what they say? 'All that glitters…'
He couldn't stop himself from sleeping
around with anything wearing knickers.

But really, he shouldn't have pushed me so far.
'I'm sorry, I can't make love anymore.
Just can't…perform.' The lying turd
was after screwing Daphne, next door…

I decided I'd give his performance a boost.
Pop a little blue pill in his tea.
How was *I* to know of his heart condition?
The pill would make him die – on me?!

Why didn't I leave him? I ask myself, now.
Why put up with it? Honest to God…
Why *be* so forgiving? Too soft in the head?
'Suppose I just loved the randy old sod…

And *he* loved me too. I *know* he did.
But now that he's dead and gone,
please, no more, *'How are you coping alone?'*
Doorbell's ringing – my new friend, John…

A Day in the Care Home

Brother and sister faced up to the fact
Dad needed round the clock care.
Memory was going, couldn't dress himself…
was chatting to people not there…

The Care Home they viewed – seeming top drawer,
was in many ways, just the ticket.
Just beyond Its gardens, a sports ground lay.
In summer, Dad could watch cricket!

They convinced themselves Dad liked the idea.
When cricket was mentioned, he smiled.
Though not really aware of where he was,
he seemed happy, just like a child.

'We'd love to have him,' the matron said.
'Why not leave him here for a day?
To see if he likes it? I'm sure he will.
A free trial with nothing to pay?'

On this crucial day, no effort was spared
to create a good impression.
Dad was given a spacious, sunny room.
'As a help against any depression.'

(Later on, he'd be moved to a tiny room
where you couldn't even swing a cat.
There'd be no more special chocolate and cakes,
though they kept very quiet about *that*.)

Whilst sitting, he leaned sharply to his left
and was quickly pushed back in his chair.
When he leaned to his right, he was pushed
back again. This seemed to him, very unfair.

'How was it, Dad?' They asked the next day,
served with teas and Bakewell Tart.
'It's not too bad, but I can't stay here.
They won't even let you fart.'

The Happy Haven

'The Happy Haven's just perfect, Mum.
There's sing-songs, games...dominoes too!
With communal living, you'll make new friends.
You'll never be bored. Always something to do...

Graham's mum just LOVES it there!
The staff, so courteous, caring, kind...
Think -- no more worries about the house...
A room of your own – and peace of mind.

Let's face it, mum, as the vicar said,
You'll be better off with round the clock care.
Beautiful gardens to sit in as well...
Coach trips to Weston-Super-Mare...'

How disappointing my only son
should turn out to be such a shit.
He clearly thinks I'm soft in the head,
a confused and brainless twit.

I've bailed him out all through his life.
How he'd love to sell my house
to pay off more of his gambling debts.
I'm no easy care-home mouse.

'All I want is for you to be happy, Mum.'
I'm staying *put.* Not born yesterday!
What a pity for him, I've just changed
my Will for our wonderful RSPCA...

From the Balcony

From the balcony of his retirement flat---
a panoramic view of the city.
Whilst he sits, enjoying his breakfast,
gone – all feelings of self-pity.

From here, he can see the bowling green.
In the distance, the church steeple.
He ponders, again, why *do* bad things
always happen to good people?

Throughout the days, his faith is strong,
but nights bring creeping doubt.
Whatever lies behind the door,
he's sure he'll soon find out.

Anyway, if there's only dust,
how would he really know?
At least, there'd be no atheist
there to say, 'I told you so.'

No matter how we use the time,
it goes, regardless of any belief…
At eighty- five, to live more years
made him sometimes feel a thief…

Enough! Away with all these thoughts.
A new day has just begun.
The forecast said no rain at all.
Straight through to evening…sun.

The Purple Suit

Whatever possessed him to wear a purple suit?
Everyone else was wearing black.
His suit was receiving a lot of attention.
This major blunder could get him the sack.

This was, after all, a menswear company
burying its founder, a great arbiter of taste
who had built his empire on dark decorum.
A *purple* suit was a waste of space!

It wouldn't have mattered at a southern funeral.
A purple suit there, fine for funeral or wake.
But *here,* they would take a very dim view.
A purple suit was a *serious* mistake.

Their looks, disapproving, no doubt about that,
all seemed to say, '*All you need is a hat.
A purple hat to match your stupid suit.*'
He was certain, now, he *would* get the boot.

But after the burial, surprise! Surprise!
People *thanked* him for being so brave!
For daring to wear purple, defying the dictator.
For making the old sod turn in his grave.

The Laughing Clown

The clown, trapped in his gilded cage,
laughed hysterically as before.
Seabirds flew by, unimpressed,
to seek a quieter distant shore...

Not for them the frantic dance
of noise from this crazed Pleasure Beach.
The desperate scramble to enjoy.
The prizes always out of reach...

Why had he returned here, now?
Simply a nostalgia trip?
A futile move to slow the flow
of time's relentless icy drip?

The Water-Chute was such a lark.
How he had loved the Noah's Ark...
Now voices mocked inside his head
from mum and dad, both long since dead.

'What is it that you hope to find?
The clock, it can't turn back.
Accept your life is in a mess.
Too late now to change tack.'

But something in the clown's strange eyes
said, 'All is not yet lost.
My laughter's here forever more
for everyone. – No cost.'

And now he knew why he'd come back.
Knew what he'd always known.
When laughter rang out from the clown
he felt far less alone.

The Mourner

Always single, he'd lived fifty years
attending no funerals at all.
This was largely due to living abroad.
Back in the UK, now having a ball

at fifty-three, he'd been to eighteen!
Funerals were coming thick and fast.
There'd been six this year. Or was it seven?
He was struggling to remember the last…

Oh yes! Frank Stubbs. (Who he actually *knew*.)
Buried in a coffin of solid oak.
An excellent buffet after the service…
Frank was always a generous bloke…

But most times, he *didn't* know them
at all. Unacquainted with the deceased,
he would do some research, then just arrive
for the service and the following feast.

At funerals, what he really enjoyed,
was getting the attention he deserved.
Someone, for a change, would listen to *him*.
A captive audience! His voice being heard

as he held forth on his favourite topics:
Ailments, pains, his general health…
He got an awful lot off his chest,
of benefit to…well, mainly himself.

But he liked to think others gained too
from simply listening to him speak.
Now, at this Wake, sitting on the loo,
he overheard two men, taking a leak:

'Who is that pathetic man rambling on?
Uninvited, don't you think?'
'I wouldn't mind betting he never knew John.
Is he lonely? Just here for a free drink?'

And then they were gone for ice cream dessert.
This really was an unwanted insight.
He paid his respects to the widow of John,
and disappeared swiftly into the night.

At the Tea Dance

'Life is like musical chairs,' his Mum said.
*'Someone's always left standing alone
without a chair when the music stops.'*
(Although she's dead, he still hears her drone…)

But why did it always have to be him?
He was still quite handsome, in a sense…
Decidedly slim, with most of his hair…
His teeth had been fixed at great expense…

His hair was silver which some women said
made him look extremely distinguished.
Whichever way you rolled the dice,
his appeal was far from extinguished.

So why had he never found a woman
to cherish until the end of his days?
Had the right one simply not come along?
Or did he need to mend his ways?

Could it possibly be that his situation
was due to him being too choosy?
Quite preposterous! Too ridiculous for words!
(The wine was making him woozy.)

The band was playing a final number.
The very last song from the singer.
Time to slip out, now, into the cold.
It made no sense to linger.

Next Friday, he would come here again,
batteries re-charged, to pursue his ideal.
Should one *particular* woman be there,
he *might* invite her out for a meal…

*'Be careful, son. Always be on your guard.
Be very selective,'* his Mum had said.
'Some women are out for all they can get…'
(He'd stayed, become her carer instead…)

But now, a different voice faintly repeated.
He listened hard, really feeling quite pissed.
*'You're dreaming. Away with the fairies, old mate.
The woman you're looking for doesn't exist.'*

Santa's Story

Passing by Santa's Christmas Grotto,
he fought against memories coming to the fore
of when he'd been a Santa himself
in this same department store.

How many years had passed since then?
His memory was hazy… tried hard to think…
Finding suitable Santas had been a problem…
Two had been sacked, both wreaking of drink…

And so, the store manager called him in.
'We need someone younger. You're just the right age.
You've worked in the toy department a year.
It's time you moved to centre stage.

Though our reputation's been tarnished somewhat
by two drunken Santas with no idea,
I'm confident you'll revive our image
as a family store and place of good cheer.

Though you'll be the youngest Santa we've had,
you'll be well disguised with beard and cap.
The kids will love your northern brogue.
You can really put this store on the map!'

The first week seemed to be going so well,
with the kids well behaved, starry eyed,
until one boy tugged very hard at the beard
which came off and there was nowhere to hide!

The boy's mum, she lodged a serious complaint.
Her son's *Santa illusion* was shattered.
The beard wasn't properly stuck on his face!
Attention to detail *mattered* !

And so, they had glued his beard firmly on.
His face had felt horribly sticky.
'We can't allow this to happen again,'
said the manager, Mr Tricky.

(Believe it or not, Tricky was his real name.)
'Just a minor setback,' He said.
'You're doing alright, son. Keep it up!'
(Santa was thinking, he'd rather be dead.)

But he'd soldiered on with pleasing success,
handing out presents galore,
until he was faced with a difficult girl
who started *screaming* for more.

Very tricky questions, like bullets were fired:
'Which computer games would he bring?'
'Where are Santa's reindeers kept?'
'Why can't we all hear Santa sing?'

On the bus home, now, he fleetingly wondered
where all those children had gone.
He smiled, ever grateful he and his wife
had decided to stop at one.

Our Neighbour's Snowman

Our neighbour's snowman had some style.
No Wurzel Gummidge nose for him.
No ancient pipe poked from his mouth.
No battered trilby from Uncle Jim.

This snowman wore a Burberry scarf,
eyes, nose and mouth of caviar.
A Panama hat, despite the cold.
From head to toe, he looked a star.

Tomorrow came and Dad was right.
Gone were the scarf and hat.
'I'm afraid son, in these difficult times,
nothing was surer than that.'

But still, the snowman looked so proud,
for at least another day.
His image, like a limpet clung,
long after he'd melted away.

Something in those caviar eyes
Spoke deeply to me and said,
'Enjoy the limelight, if it comes.
You're a very long time dead.'

Black Cats

In parts of Britain, other countries too,
some say it's lucky to spot black cats.
'Oh look! A black cat crossed my path!'
Are these people wiser or silly prats?

Where did this notion come from, then?
Why do people believe in this?
Whoever came up with this idea?
Was he or she merely taking the piss?

True, one was owned by King Charles 1st.
It was cherished and loved beyond reason.
When the cat died, the King's luck ran out,
arrested, beheaded for treason.

But some countries take a different view.
Black cats are considered bad luck.
In the USA, France and India too,
they have come very badly unstuck.

Pope Gregory IX condemned the black cat
as Satan's incarnation.
They've had a poor press ever since
this 1232 Declaration.

But, speaking as a neutral Tom
whose coat is white and brown,
as their females give me lots of…treats,
I'm *delighted* they're still around.

The Grand Old Duke of York Nursery Rhyme Revisited

What to make of the Grand Old Duke?
Was he really so very grand?
Marching ten thousand men up a hill?
Why did he issue this strange command?

Why did he order his men to do this?
Was it simply to keep them fit?
An exercise to toughen them up,
making them march up in full kit?

Of course, he never marched up, himself.
No, he rode on his horse, named Ned.
After taking the duke to the top of the hill,
the poor horse, he dropped down dead.

It has to be said, there's a darker view.
A latent sadistic streak?
Did the Duke get his kicks from inflicting pain?
From making strong men weak?

'Nonsense!' The duke's supporters claim.
'Just malicious tittle-tattle!
Much better to lead his men up a hill
than into some crazy battle.

In doing so, the duke tried to save lives,
delaying the slaughter ahead.'
Did a love of humanity really prevail?
Or was he just sick in the head?

POEMS AUTOBIOGRAPHICAL?
Written during Lockdown, March 2020 – 2021

The Magpies

Don't Buy a Hamster for Your Son

Blackpool Stop Off

Back Down to Earth

1958

Listen with Mother

Saying Sorry to Miss Green

Death of a Corner Shop

The Chair

Mister Willis

1970

The Purple Pussycat

The Poetry Reading

Look Back in Anguish

Ode to Ralph Gubbins

The Magpies

Sipping wine, I watch two magpies on our lawn.
A good omen, I'm certain. Two for joy?
I watch them regally strutting their stuff.
What will we have? A girl or a boy?

Of course, we could have known in advance
our baby's sex before it came.
Our friends all knew what clothes to buy.
Nothing like being ahead of the game?

But we decided to wait and see.
Nothing beats a surprise, we thought.
'The baby's kicking!' I hear you yell.
A footballer? Or an astronaut?

'The baby's kicking! Has very strong legs!'
A swimmer or gymnast if it's a girl…
Or perhaps she could be a soccer star!
An all-rounder, giving all three a whirl!

But now I see one magpie's vanished,
leaving *one*. What does *this* mean?
One for sorrow? Give me a break!
I think I need a change of scene.

This wine I'm drinking's far too strong.
This magpie business is a load of crap.
Truth is, I'm feeling rather sloshed.
I think I'll go and take a nap.

Don't Buy a Hamster for Your Son

Don't buy a hamster for your son.
A hamster's life is very brief.
Exhausted on their hamster wheels,
they drop dead early, causing grief.

My son had five. (Not all at once.)
All died within two years.
Our garden was a cemetery.
Our house, a vale of tears.

But please don't think, *all doom and gloom*.
There was some fun as well.
Despite the many tales of woe,
it wasn't *always* hell.

The most difficult hamster of them all?
Without doubt, number three.
He hid in our kitchen for several days.
We couldn't just let him be...

We simply had to flush him out.
Return him to his abode.
On this, we were very strongly advised
to follow '*The Hamster Code.*'

So, with three bricks, we made small steps
to the top of a plastic bucket.
Squeezed carrot juice upon the steps.
Number three would smell and suck it.

Then, climbing up, he'd see the carrot
in the bucket, ready to eat.
Once in his 'prison', he couldn't escape.
His capture would be complete!

Next morning, great! This trick had worked.
Trapped in the bucket, as they said!
Everyone was as pleased as Punch,
until – soon after – number three dropped dead!

The point is, hamsters *hate* being outwitted.
That's *another* thing about them, see?
Poor losers. They just *can't* handle defeat.
They would rather *die!* It's all *Me! Me!*

Don't buy a hamster for your son.
It'll only make him blue.
Why not buy a tortoise instead?
They live to a hundred and two!

Blackpool Stop – Off

'How about having a day in Blackpool?
Could just stop off as it's on our way?
An hour on the beach? Maybe visit the Tower?
Years since we've been there. What do you say?'

Blackpool! He'd been there lots as a kid.
How he used to love The Golden Mile!
The Kentucky Derby, the Pleasure Beach…
The Hall of Mirrors always made him smile…

'Okay, let's do it,' he heard himself say.
(He'd been driving three hours and needed a leak.)
'We'll really relax on the beach,' his wife said.
'Breathe in the sea air. Have Bubble and Squeak.'

'Oh no! Not in *Blackpool!'* he heard himself shout.
'It's *famous* for fish and chips!'
The thought of this really did spur him on.
It'd been so long…he was licking his lips.

And so, they arrived and lay on the beach.
How happy he was with his little band!
His son and daughter, in their early teens…
His wife, still the prettiest girl in the land…

'Just savour the moment,' he told himself.
How lovely again, to see the sea!
Alas, as he dozed, his wife's voice, shrill:
'Your son has just been stung by a bee!'

Ten minutes later, his daughter cried,
'My contact lense fell out!
It's got to be here in the sand, somewhere…'
Stay calm, he thought. Don't shout.

So, getting down on hands and knees,
under the pitiless sun,
they searched and sifted through the sand.
In vain. The sand had won.

Then off they went for fish and chips,
too hot, too tired to speak.
Only to find the chip shop closed.
Re-opening the following week.

'Whose idea *was* it to stop?' He barked.
His wife, well she just sighed,
'It seemed a good idea at the time…
You thought so, too!' she cried.

The slings and arrows of outrageous fortune
had rained down on his head.
It really had been one of those days.
He should have stayed in bed.

But as he drove to their destination,
he was certain of one thing, at least:
No matter how hungry he was for the past,
he would never return for the feast.

Back Down to Earth

Today his son was seven years old.
Amongst the presents, a new football.
He suggested a kick about in the garden.
'But be careful. Don't kick it over the wall.'

Sure enough, after five minutes play,
The ball ended up in his neighbour's back yard.
Whilst showing his son the best way to head,
he headed the ball too high and too hard.

'Don't worry,' he said, standing on the wall,
'I'll get it, then I'll show you the knack
of accurate heading. Of heading the ball ---'
Now golden memories came flooding back…

When young, he'd been famous as a local player
for giving opposing defenses hell.
So fast! With wonderful poise and flair…
Now, from the top of the wall, he fell.

'Mum! Dad's fallen!' He heard his son yell.
'I'm alright!' He lied. Quite a bad ankle sprain…
Somehow, he scrambled back over the wall,
trying hard to conceal his anger and pain.

'Your dad was good at football, once,' mum said.
His son pulled a face, said, *'Wow.'*
'Your dad was a striker. Scored lots of goals.'
Then he heard his son say, *'He's useless, now.'*

1958

'Alright! That's it! I'm going to the police!'
A familiar threat from Mr Sweet,
trying to stop our football match
in front of his house on a carless street.

Off to the police station he would go.
(Or so he would have us think.
He only went to the corner pub.)
'They're coming!' he'd shout, after having a drink.

Not born yesterday, we were *ten* years old!
To play at Wembley – our greatest dream.
Bolton Wanderers had just won the FA Cup!
One day, we would *all* play in their team!

Of course, *other* things happened in '58.
Sir Edmund Hillary reached The South Pole...
The Everly Brothers sang, 'Claudette'
In America, thousands thrown on the dole...

Donald Campbell's record for water speed...
CND. Ten thousand in Trafalgar Square.
The ending of coal rationing finally announced.
The first published edition of Paddington Bear...

But, for us boys, the main questions were:
When will our parents buy us a bike?
Pay for the cinema *every* week?
Let us go fishing for Bream and Pike?

Mr Sweet's long gone and Mrs Sweet, too.
There's not the same urge for football fame.
Instead, young boys in their bedrooms, sit,
playing the latest computer game.

But, sometimes, in my seventies, now,
I see one boy still there.
The houses looking much the same.
No cars. The street still bare.

He's playing football on his own.
'Where are your friends?' I cry.
They're gone for good. I'll join them soon,
play football in the sky.

Listen with Mother

When I was six, Mum said to me,
'There's no percentage in being bad.'
When I asked her what a percentage was,
she said, *'You'd better ask your dad.*

If you're bad, they'll come and take you away.'
'Where will they take me?' I wanted to know.
'If you don't eat all your carrots up,
they'll take you where you don't want to go.

And if you fall whilst climbing that tree
and break your leg, don't come running to me.
I'm not like your teacher, Mr Ted.
Haven't got eyes in the back of my head.'

I stared at the head of Mr Ted,
but his head only had two eyes.
There must be more. Mum said there were.
And Mums didn't tell boys lies…

Her jumble sale of words survive,
a fractured echo from above,
the world outside my window still
a fearful mix of threat and love.

Saying Sorry to Miss Green

We're sorry Miss Green. If we'd only known
what you were going through,
we would have done our very best
to stop you feeling blue.

If we'd seen inside your head,
us kids, all eight years old,
would have been so well behaved
and done as we were told.

But now's too late. 'Can't blame the class.'
Well, so say mum and dad.
'Her life went wrong too many times
to make her feel *so* sad…'

We hope you've found peace, now, Miss Green.
Didn't mean to make you cry.
Some grown-ups say you've gone
to teach small angels in the sky.

Death of a Corner Shop

'There's too many customers stealing chocolate
from the counter of this shop.'
Dad hung a large mirror on the wall,
hoping this would make them stop.

As we lived behind in the small back room,
I soon gazed into the mirror, too.
(Not *really* looking for people who steal.)
No, thinking back -- just for something to do.

Looking at the mirror into the shop
provided theatre of a kind,
northern folk talking with their hands,
gossip and stories, springing to mind.

'Did you hear Joan Webster's pregnant again?
She's not sure if it's Derek or Bill.'
'Hanging from bannisters, when he was found,
but I understand he'd been very ill...'

'And what about Mrs Daley's son?
Burnt his boats, no doubt about that.
'He's gone to prison for violent assault.'
'Mrs Evans spent eighty pounds on a hat!'

Like the houses around, the shop's boarded, now,
a bulldozer poised to wipe out the past
to be replaced by a block of flats,
a Macdonald's, Tesco – the dye is cast.

Runner Up. March 2021.
The Harrow Times Poetry Competition.

The Chair

You caught my eye again today,
still by the window, tired, forlorn.
My father's favourite chair, once proud,
now stained and shabby, fabric worn.

No one ever sits on you now.
You're just a waste of space.
Our other chairs are sparkling new.
You're just a huge disgrace.

What would father make of you now?
My guess is he'd give you the elbow.
Forsake you. Ditch you in two minutes flat
for our leather recliner from Malmo.

Oh, please don't give me your sorry look!
Your sad, self-pitying gaze.
Cheer up! You're seating Guy Fawkes soon.
Going out in a glorious blaze!

How many chairs end life like that?
Think of all the reflected glory:
You'll die, still working, in one piece.
Alright, so it may seem gory...

But the plain fact is—don't make a scene ---
You *know* we all have to die.
The longer I stare at you, selfish chair,
I see him there, and cry.

Okay, I guess you win again,
but let's just get this clear:
This is your very *last* reprieve.
Your *last one.* Do you hear?

Mr Willis

Everyone living in the street agreed,
Mr Willis was a very strange man.
He lived a peculiar life indeed.
His attitude no one could understand.

He never took part in mischievous talk,
never went out except for his walk
which he always took at quarter to two.
Where he walked to, nobody knew.

To us kids, he was a miser. A man of wealth
going somewhere to count his silver and gold.
The grown-ups said, *'He lives on the state,*
claiming benefits for just having a cold !

And his house is rank. A complete disgrace.
Not even fit for an animal, now.'
Though I couldn't see through – his curtains were drawn –
I could never believe he kept a cow,

but some said he did. They'd heard it mooing.
'It was chained to the kitchen sink,' they said.
'I've seen it!' claimed the woman next door.
'It's brown and white and he calls it, Ned.'

The bottom line was, his house was to blame
in the street for lowering the tone.
'Our houses will never command their right price
because of him,' was the general moan.

So, next, they tried to hound him
out of his house to a council flat.
The pressure was growing on him to move,
but then he dropped dead, so that was that!

Or so they thought…Still their houses didn't sell.
The market collapsed when recession came.
I was there last week, thirty years further on,
The houses…they looked just the same.

Mum and dad are buried nearby.
Lots of our neighbours are buried there, too.
His grave's as neat and proper as theirs.
The words on his stone as brief and true.

1970

'Nice to see you. When are you going back?'
A northern greeting I grew to know well
on my first visit home since moving away.
'How are you finding the cockneys, Mel?'

'How are you finding London?' asked dad.
'How much is a pint of beer?
Remember, you can always come back.'
Great words of comfort I *needed* to hear.

1970. I was twenty-two.
'Mr Bloe' was number one in the charts.
Harold Wilson had been defeated by Ted.
Filkins won the Championship Darts.

The Jumbo Jet went into service.
Concord's first supersonic flight...
The biggest blues and rock show ever
was taking place on The Isle of Wight.

Hendrix and Janis Joplin passed on.
A mighty earthquake shook Peru.
The Beatles were singing 'Let It Be.'
President Nasser passed on too.

1970. Police Walkie Talkies.
No mobile phones or internet.
No segregation of football fans.
And very little student debt.

When I was small, – two crucial questions:
Will we ever get a man on the moon?
Will we be able to make a phone call,
seeing the person we're speaking to, soon?

In '69 men *had* walked on the moon.
Quite a while later, skyping began.
Technology's triumphed at every turn.
Could it, someday, even *dignify* man?

...

Well, things worked out, I'm pleased to report.
My move to London proved a success.
But, look, aren't you tired of this reminiscing?
What's that, you say? *'Now there's far less stress?'*

I'm not so sure, but I'll take your word.
Okay? I won't argue at all.
The past is gone. Let's leave it there.
Was life better? – Too close to call.

The Purple Pussycat

Weary of Central London Discos,
he asked, *'Are there any outside the West End?'*
His then workmate, Colin, said, *'Quite a few.*
But only one, would I recommend.

Try the Purple Pussycat, Finchley Road.
You'll find it's a pretty cool place.
Don't let the name of it put you off.
The 'Pussycat' is a really cool space.'

Everyone used the word, 'cool' a lot,
In '72 this word was in vogue.
(Colin was sacked the following week
for being a very light-fingered rogue.)

But off he went, on Colin's advice,
to check this *cool* place out.
Although he danced with two gorgeous girls,
he was never in with a shout.

He drew a blank. Other guys got lucky
as the evening wore on. Not him.
He really was getting nowhere at all.
It was late. Things were looking grim.

He glanced again at the girl, on her own,
who had turned down each request to dance
from ten men at least, or even more.
Why bother asking? He had *no* chance.

Who *was* she? He wondered. This mystery girl?
The loveliest in the room by a mile.
Whoever she was, he'd left it too late.
As he turned to leave, he saw her smile…

And *then* he thought, oh what the hell?
There's nothing to lose. It's the last dance, right?
Against all odds, she agreed to dance
and to a date the following night!

…

She lived at the end of the Northern Line.
All the way out to Edgware, he went.
He remembered, thinking, *I must be mad!*
This is almost as far as going to Kent!

They'd arranged to meet at Edgware Station.
Already, she was seriously late.
He'd been strung along! She was standing him up!
How stupid to have made this date…

But then she arrived in her Fiat 500,
drove them out to a country pub.
The Coach and Horses in Elstree, it was…
A candle lit dinner – *very* good grub…

For forty-five years, they've been man and wife.
He loves her dearly. She still loves him.
He wonders where the time has gone…
Two grandchildren, now…little Carla and Tim…

Sometimes he thinks of Colin, too…
Jailed for murdering some diplomat…
Unaware of the joy he'd helped to bring,
recommending The Purple Pussycat.

The Poetry Reading

He would comb his hair differently tonight.
Like Dylan Thomas, he would wear a bow.
He stared in the mirror, liked what he saw.
He was looking good. Nearly time to go.

His appearance had been achieved with great care.
Although rumpled, his clothes had subdued panache.
He looked, every inch, the experienced poet.
Should he change his shoes? No! Really must dash.

He was off to a *serious* poetry event.
Alright. So, change your shoes, then go!
His reputation was much at stake,
reading two of his poems to open the show.

It *was* important for him to *look* good.
At all costs, he must look the part,
nonchalant, but not *too* laid back...
slightly disheveled...casual but smart.

Arriving at The Civic Hall
where the readings were to take place,
all poets were told they were on their own.
The Compere was drunk. A complete disgrace!

This now meant doing his own introduction,
adjusting the mic all by himself.
He could *never* adjust them to the right height...
Mics were a *threat* to his mental health!

Sods Law. The poet, on stage before him,
had been very short. Only five feet tall.
Try as he may, he couldn't budge the mic...
He had to shrink, somehow. Make himself small...

So, he read the first poem, very crouched,
speaking into the mic, bent at the knees.
The audience, thinking this part of his act,
laughing out loud. He was far from pleased.

...

He regarded himself as a serious poet,
used to commanding a certain respect.
For his fans, admirers in the audience tonight,
this *wasn't* what they'd come to expect.

Having no option, he had to continue.
He fiddled with the mic once more.
This time it shot up above his head!
He wanted to disappear through the floor.

He had no option now the mic was stuck…
He read the next poem, stood on a chair.
Did they *really* think this part of his act
as they carried on laughing? *Great Despair!!*

But once it was over, he had to admit
the applause seemed much greater tonight.
Could his reputation be salvaged at all?
Well, he *wouldn't* go down without a fight!

Then the Manager of The Civic Centre
came to him, shook him by the hand.
'You're the best comedian we've ever had!
Your timing's perfect. Your delivery…grand.

We would like you to appear again
next week on our brand-new comedy show.
We've been searching for a fun novelty act.
Will you think about it and let me know?'

Look Back in Anguish

The London Lunchtime Theatre scene
was booming in nineteen seventy-one.
He'd managed to write his very first play
and had now been told it was going on!

He'd also been given an Arts Council Grant
to support his half hour play.
What a wonderful start to his playwriting career!
Everything seemed to be going his way.

The production sold out in no time at all.
This meant the actors would raise their game.
Sure, the tiny theatre seated *forty- two*,
but playing to *forty* was almost the same…

It was going so well! The audience, rapt.
To see his play come alive was a thrill!
The acting, direction - both without fault.
His writing? Well, way above run of the mill…

But after twenty minutes, an audience member
got up and simply stormed out the door.
My God! He thought. This is catastrophic!
His confidence was shaken to the core.

He wanted to yell, '*Come back! Come back*!
You can't do this! It's my very first play!'
If I can't hold attention for twenty minutes,
he thought, I might as well call it a day.

But afterwards, people told him, '*Don't worry.
The man who stormed out's not a critical jerk.
He only gets thirty-five minutes for lunch
and always leaves early to get back to work.*'

Ode to Ralph Gubbins

(Bolton V Blackburn FA Cup Semi Final 1958)

Nat Lofthouse couldn't play in the semi final,
having been injured the previous match.
Ralph Gubbins was chosen to stand in for Nat.
Some people said, *'Gubbins ain't up to scratch.*

Selecting Ralph Gubbins makes no kind of sense.
He's no centre forward. Plays best near the wing.
He's no chance at all against Blackburn's defense.
He's the wrong replacement for Nat, our King.

Too fragile. Too artful. They'll just squeeze him out.
He's a very fine player but lacking Nat's clout.'
Others said, *'We must all get behind the team.*
Give Ralph a fair chance to deliver our dream.'
But the chorus from doubters was growing quite loud.
Ralph had a great deal to prove to the crowd.

So, against this background, semi final day came.
Eighty thousand crammed in for the game.
Stood on a small stool made specially by dad –
I was nine years old and football mad.

Blackburn started well, scored the first goal.
Then to make matters worse, it started to rain.
As we put on our hooded plastic macs,
our ragged team looked like losing the game.

After much shouting, we got sore throats.
Dad said, *'Here, suck on this Locket.'*
As I took it, I spotted the man next to dad,
peeing in someone's pocket!

Looking back, I *know* I should have told dad.
But I found I just couldn't speak.
By the time I managed to open my mouth,
the man had finished his leak.

And Bolton had scored! A Ralph Gubbins goal!
Which, being distracted, I missed.
But all was forgiven when Ralph scored again
and then I was being hugged and kissed.

Being kissed by dad! We had won two-one!
The Bolton fans were ecstatic!
To come from behind through Gubbins's goals
made victory more sweetly emphatic.

Bolton won the final, Nat lifting the cup,
having scored twice against Man U.
But Bolton wouldn't have been in the final
at all had Ralph not scored his two.

'We can be heroes,' goes the David Bowie song.
'We can be heroes just for one day.'
Ralph Gubbins is a hero forever more
even though, the final, he didn't get to play.

THREE POEMS WRITTEN BEFORE LOCKDOWN – 2019

When The Beatles came to Brent

Landslide for Boris

This be the Verse (Alternative version of the Philip Larkin poem)

When the Beatles Came to Brent

April '63. Great excitement in Brent!
The Beatles were coming! Seemed heaven sent!
They were doing a show at The Gaumont State.
All my friends were ecstatic. Just couldn't wait

to hear the fab four sing in all their glory.
How they got tickets was another story.
Let's move on, shall we? Get tickets, they did.
When The Beatles are playing, what's a few quid?

My friend, Doreen got a spare ticket for me
but I told her I'd seen them on TV,
could do *without* all the screaming and noise.
Besides, my main interest was dating boys…
I didn't really need George, Paul, Ringo and John.
They were lovely but not as lovely as Ron…

Well, after the show, Doreen couldn't speak.
She had lost her voice through screaming.
I remember feeling a little bit smug;
but I wasn't exactly beaming.

The show was forever the talk of the street.
All my friends crowed, '*You missed a real treat* !'
Wouldn't let me forget it. I wish I *had* gone…
Later on, I got a big crush for John…
The Beatles went mega soon after this event
and they never came back to play in Brent.

Written on request for the East Lane Theatre Company
as part of The Brent Year of Culture celebrations.

Landslide for Boris

A Boris Landslide. Lots of landslides before.
There's no telling where this landslide will lead.
Independent glory? A Britain, revived?
Or into a rut of austerity and need?

The country's divided on Brexit for sure.
Half the people unhappy, however it may go.
Split down the middle, the newspapers say.
A tale of joy or a tale of woe?

Well, good luck to Boris. Sooner him than me.
Will he weave a magic spell
to heal a country, split and torn?
Or plunge us into a deeper hell?

23rd July 2019. Tory Leadership Result amidst Brexit.

This Be the Verse

(Alternative version to the Philip Larkin Poem)

They boost you up, your mum and dad.
May not mean to, but they do.
Although you inherit *a few* of their faults,
you inherit *many* of their good points too.

I like to think they were boosted in turn
by parents in old style hats and coats
who also raised them with loving concern,
advising them always to never burn boats.

Man hands on opportunities to man.
Consider them all but be true to yourself.
And should you have kids, make sure you can
be there for them always through sickness and health.

Written as an exercise for The Pinner Writers Group.